THE MYSTERY OF KITSUNE SHRINE

A.K.MOHAMMED RIDWAN

Copyright © A.K.Mohammed Ridwan
All Rights Reserved.

This book has been self-published with all reasonable efforts taken to make the material error-free by the author. No part of this book shall be used, reproduced in any manner whatsoever without written permission from the author, except in the case of brief quotations embodied in critical articles and reviews.

The Author of this book is solely responsible and liable for its content including but not limited to the views, representations, descriptions, statements, information, opinions and references ["Content"]. The Content of this book shall not constitute or be construed or deemed to reflect the opinion or expression of the Publisher or Editor. Neither the Publisher nor Editor endorse or approve the Content of this book or guarantee the reliability, accuracy or completeness of the Content published herein and do not make any representations or warranties of any kind, express or implied, including but not limited to the implied warranties of merchantability, fitness for a particular purpose. The Publisher and Editor shall not be liable whatsoever for any errors, omissions, whether such errors or omissions result from negligence, accident, or any other cause or claims for loss or damages of any kind, including without limitation, indirect or consequential loss or damage arising out of use, inability to use, or about the reliability, accuracy or sufficiency of the information contained in this book.

Made with ♥ on the Notion Press Platform
www.notionpress.com

Contents

Preface

Hi there, I'm Mohammed Ridwan, Son of A.S.Abul Kalam and S.R.Riyas Banu. I am a budding 14-year-old author. I was born in 2010, Tamil Nadu district in India. This book marks the beginning of my writing journey, and I'm thrilled to share it with you. As a young writer, I wanted to create a story that would captivate readers of all ages, especially young adults like myself, with its blend of fantasy and adventure.One unique aspect of this book is that it contains no images. Instead, I've left the descriptions open-ended, allowing readers to envision the characters and scenes in their own imaginative way. I believe this adds a personal touch to the reading experience, making it more immersive and engaging.Born on 12th February 2010, I've always had a passion for storytelling and creative writing. This book is a testament to my love for crafting compelling narratives that transport readers to new and exciting worlds.n this book, you'll embark on an adventure with Julia and Jackson, two daring adventurers who find themselves unraveling the mystery of a prehistoric creature in modern times. Their journey is filled with twists and turns, danger and discovery, as they race against time to uncover the truth.I hope you enjoy reading this book as much as I enjoyed writing it. Thank you for joining me on this thrilling literary adventure!

Prologue

In the bustling city of California, two siblings, Julia and Jackson, found themselves drawn together by fate. Julia, at 17, was the protective older sister, wise beyond her years, with a fierce determination to look after her younger brother. Jackson, just 15, was the adventurous younger brother, with a curiosity that often led them into exciting—and sometimes dangerous—situations. Despite their differences, they shared a deep bond and an unbreakable resolve to face whatever challenges came their way. Little did they know, their greatest adventure was about to unfold.

The Screams in the Morning

Julia and Jackson were two professional adventurers at just the age below 20 years old with Julia being 17 and Jackson being 15 years old. They were even awarded many prizes for the extraordinary adventures they did. Julia and Jackson, despite their young age, shared an unbreakable bond as siblings. Julia, being the older sister, took on the role of protector and caregiver for Jackson. She always made sure he was safe during their adventures, keeping a watchful eye on him at all times. Whether they were traversing treacherous terrain or braving dangerous challenges, Julia's priority was always her brother's well-being. In return, Jackson looked up to his sister with admiration and trust. He knew he could rely on Julia for guidance and support in any situation. Even though he was the younger sibling, Jackson often showed his appreciation by assisting Julia whenever he could, whether it was carrying equipment or providing moral support during tough times. Their relationship was built on a foundation of mutual respect and love, strengthened by the shared experiences of their adventurous endeavors. Despite the risks they faced,

Julia and Jackson knew they could count on each other, making their bond as siblings an essential aspect of their success in the world of professional adventuring. One stormy evening during an expedition through the dense jungle, Julia suddenly found herself trapped beneath a fallen tree branch, injured and unable to move. Rain poured down relentlessly, making visibility poor and the ground slippery. Despite Julia's attempts to free herself, the weight of the branch pinned her down, causing her pain with every movement. As panic started to set in, Jackson, with the strength of a bull, immediately sprang into action. With adrenaline coursing through his veins, he assessed the situation swiftly, determined to rescue his sister. Ignoring the rain pelting down on him, Jackson braced himself against the trunk of the fallen tree, muscles bulging as he exerted all his might.

With a mighty heave, Jackson managed to lift the heavy branch just enough for Julia to wiggle free. Despite the strain and exhaustion, he didn't falter, his only focus was on ensuring Julia's safety. With his sister finally out of harm's way, Jackson's relief was palpable, his heart pounding with a mix of adrenaline and gratitude for being able to protect his elder sister. Julia, though injured, couldn't help but feel a swell of pride and gratitude towards her younger brother. She knew she could always count on Jackson's strength and determination, just as he could count on her guidance and support. This moment served as a powerful reminder of their unbreakable bond as siblings, forged through the trials and triumphs of their adventurous endeavors.

While walking home one evening, the air was filled with the usual sounds of the city—cars honking, people chatting, and the distant hum of life. Suddenly, a bloodcurdling scream pierced the air, causing them to stop in their tracks. They exchanged glances of concern and hurried toward the direction of the sound, their curiosity piqued. Pushing through the crowded streets, they arrived at a dimly lit alley where the scream had originated. What they saw next would change their lives forever. In the shadows, a figure was crouched over something, emitting guttural noises that sent shivers down their spines. As they cautiously approached, they realized the figure was a woman, her face contorted in fear. But what lay in front of her was unlike anything they had ever seen. It was a creature straight out of a history book, a creature that should have been extinct for millions of years—a Kitsune. Its scales glinted in the dim light, its claws sharp and menacing. Julia and Jackson's hearts pounded in their chests as they stared, transfixed, at the impossible sight before them. The creature let out another low growl, causing the woman to whimper in terror. Julia, always the protector, stepped forward, her voice surprisingly steady despite the fear coursing through her veins. "Hey, leave her alone!" she called out, hoping to distract the creature. To their surprise, the creature turned its attention towards them, its eyes narrowing in curiosity. Jackson, feeling a surge of bravery, stood beside his sister, ready to defend her if necessary. The creature regarded them for a moment, its gaze surprisingly intelligent. Then, with a sudden movement, it turned and bounded away, disappearing into the darkness. Julia and Jackson watched in awe as it disappeared from view, unable to comprehend what they had just witnessed. The woman, now free from the creature's gaze, scrambled to her feet and ran towards them, her eyes wide with fear. "Thank you," she gasped, her voice trembling. "I don't know what that thing was, But I am shivering my timbers. (not really tho lol)". Julia and Jackson exchanged a glance, their minds racing with questions. What was that creature? How did it come to be here, in their city? And most importantly, what did its presence mean for the world as they knew it?

As they walked home, their minds buzzing with thoughts, Julia and Jackson couldn't shake the feeling that their lives were about to change in ways they never could have imagined.

The next day, Julia and Jackson couldn't stop thinking about the creature they had encountered. They spent hours researching, scouring the internet for any information that could shed light on its origins. Eventually, they stumbled upon an article that made their blood run cold. According to the article, several other sightings of similar creatures have been reported in different parts of the world. Scientists were baffled, unable to explain how these ancient creatures had suddenly reappeared after millions of years of extinction. Theories ranged from time travel experiments gone wrong to hidden pockets of prehistoric land that had somehow survived beneath the earth's surface. Julia and Jackson were fascinated and terrified in equal measure. They knew they had to learn more, but they also knew they were way over their heads. They decided to seek out the help of someone who could guide them in their quest for answers.

George, a slim-haired man and an uncle of those two with eyes as blue as the sky, joined forces with Julia and Jackson since they insisted him to help them solve a mysterious series of events. Despite being 38 years old, George had a playful and childish demeanor, often surprising Julia and Jackson with his unconventional ideas. As they investigated, they noticed they were being followed, sparking their curiosity. Their first clue came when they discovered that a wealthy man named Mike had recently moved to the city. Initially dismissing this as trivial, they soon realized its significance when they saw Mike's wife, the woman they had seen that morning. Sensing a connection to a larger case, they delved deeper into the mystery, exploring the possibility of a hidden agenda behind Mike's relocation. However, this only raised more questions, particularly about the awakening of a Kitsune, a creature from a million years past, and why it had not attacked them earlier. Julia, being a responsible sister, initially advised Jackson to stay back, but he insisted on joining the team under the condition that he be cautious. The investigation led them from California to Europe, where Mike had previously resided. Discovering that Mike had moved due to significant business losses, they hit a dead end. But their perseverance paid off when Jackson suggested investigating Mike's wife, Sarah, who turned out to be from India, with her father being a Military General in the Indian army. This new lead opened up a world of possibilities, hinting at a deeper, more complex mystery that they were determined to unravel. But one question, Why didn't they ask the woman directly? (Maybe ask her?). They researched India and found out that a shrine of prehistoric creatures was found 4 months back. It was the shrine of none other but the "Kitsune".

CHAPTER TWO

Search for the animal.

The kitsune shrine showed its structure as a picture designed with natural paints, its sleek body bathed in an ethereal shade of blue, its eyes as dark as the night sky, yet striking with five vibrant stripes of red and black. It was a sight rarely seen, a creature of mystery and allure. In California, sightings of such a kitsune with red eyes had sparked fear and speculation. Julia and Jackson, siblings on an adventure, felt a shiver run down their spines as they sensed they were being followed. Their instincts were right; an arrow laced with poison whizzed past Julia, narrowly missing her. Despite his young age, Jackson possessed a strength that rivaled that of a bull. When the assailant attempted to flee, Jackson chased him down and apprehended him. Pressed for answers, the mysterious man triggered a timer on his gold watch, setting off a countdown of only five seconds. In a moment of quick thinking, Julia shielded her brother, but the watch turned out to be a bomb.

Thanks to their friend George, a brilliant scientist who remotely disabled the bomb, disaster was averted. As they tried to make sense of the situation, the man managed to escape, but BAAM! The sound came, someone had detonated the bomb remotely. This made them realize they were not dealing with a lone villain but an entire nefarious organization. The chase had only just begun. But why were they chasing them? Why were they trying to kill them? As they ran towards the helicopter they had used to come to India, the stone plates beneath them suddenly started shaking. George sensed that this could be a second trap by the villain team, so he quickly rushed everyone to seek cover under the stone statue of the kitsune placed on top of the shrine. Just as he suspected, a missile hit the helicopter, causing a fiery explosion. Jackson's hand was slightly injured in the chaos. Moments later, a roaring sound filled the air, and to their surprise, the kitsune appeared, its eyes glowing red, standing next to the wreckage. It began to run towards them, clearly intent on hunting them down. Acting swiftly, the group decided to flee towards the nearby state of Madhya Pradesh, which was about 4 to 6 kilometers away. Finally reaching the city's entrance after a long run, they were relieved to find that the kitsune was nowhere to be seen. Realizing they needed to act fast, they quickly entered the city and headed to a local library to research the creature. There, they discovered a heavily guarded book titled "The History Behind the Madness of Kitsune." Thanks to George's reputation as a well-known scientist, they were granted permission to borrow the book for the next 72 hours, giving them a crucial opportunity to uncover the truth and confront the creature.

CHAPTER THREE

Kitsune's Origin

Julia started screaming "THIS BOOK IS WRITTEN IN SANSKRIPT".Jackson thought she didn't know it and he said: "Aww look how confused she is".Then Julia said, "I shouted because I know Sanskript, and it's one of my favorite languages too".It was like Jackson's nose was broken. (Bro got emotional damage lol). Then she started reading the book.

In ancient times, the kitsune was revered as a benevolent and divine creature, embodying wisdom, protection, and good fortune. Tales of the kitsune's noble deeds and miraculous feats were cherished, and passed down through generations, ingraining it deeply in the hearts of the people.

Legends spoke of the kitsune as a guardian spirit, tirelessly watching over the forests, safeguarding them from harm. It was believed that the kitsune's presence brought blessings of prosperity and fertility to those who showed it respect and reverence.

Yet, as with many legends, some sought to manipulate the truth for their nefarious ends. Over time, stories emerged of kitsune using their powers for mischief and deceit, sowing chaos wherever they roamed.

These darker tales spread like wildfire, tarnishing the kitsune's once pristine reputation. People began to fear the kitsune, viewing it as a bringer of misfortune and disaster. The creature, once revered, became a symbol of mistrust and treachery, shunned by those who had once honored it.

Despite this shift in perception, some clung to the belief in the kitsune's true nature. They understood that the kitsune was not inherently evil but had been corrupted by the greed and malice of others. These believers sought to uncover the truth behind the kitsune's fall from grace, striving to restore its honor and reputation.

The legend of the kitsune endures as a cautionary tale, a reminder of the dangers of allowing fear and ignorance to guide our actions. It stands as a testament to the enduring power of hope and redemption, even in the face of darkness.

As Julia looked over, she noticed that both Georgie and Jackson had fallen asleep. Suddenly, a growling sound filled the air, startling them awake. It was Julia, playfully trying to rouse them. Jackson, still half-asleep, jokingly pulled her hair, sparking a playful scuffle between them. Amidst the laughter, Julia shared the tale of the kitsune, how it had once been a symbol of goodness but had been twisted by the actions of others. She explained that the kitsune they had encountered was not the real kitsune, as its true nature remained pure, its color unchanged by its emotions.

Georgie and Jackson listened intently, amazed by the revelation. Jackson whispered in awe, "So, the kitsune we saw was not the real kitsune?" The mystery deepened, adding another layer of intrigue to their adventure.

Realizing they needed more information, they decided to return to the shrine for further investigation. However, in their haste to leave the library, they forgot to return the borrowed book. The observant library owner noticed and dispatched four guards to retrieve it. Oblivious to the situation, they boarded a bus. The guards, unable to locate them, returned to the owner empty-handed. Remembering that they still had three days before the book was due, the owner decided to let it slide, knowing George's responsible nature. This incident served as a reminder to always be mindful of your surroundings and responsibilities.

They went to a hotel to stay since it was midnight. (If this was me dude I would've just slept, to be honest). They researched about Mike and his wife Sarah in their Windows 8 laptop with a 10th-generation processor. (Probably Jackson must be a gamer if I guess.)While doing so they slept. George had to sleep on the couch. In the morning George got up early and found the brother and sister duo missing. For a second he thought they went without him. But they went outside and brought some coffee for the three of them. The team had some coffee and started their journey toward the shrine. After getting there, they started to investigate the area. George while investigating the statue finds a small button below its body very hidden. He tries to press the button but it looks like it needs some type of shape to fit on it. George being a scientist took out a small 3D Printer which scanned that pattern and started to print. After 4 hours the shape was ready to be fitted in. After fitting the shape it opened up a small area that had a stone. They thought the stone was just a normal one. But Jackson insisted on keeping it since it looked very old. After collecting it they decided to investigate more. Suddenly Julia saw a small shiny substance near the Statue but not very close. They started digging in the soil and found a bomb. George being a scientist, knew what type was it and realised a tag under it. Before going they diffused the bomb and went looking for the one who made it. The tag had the name "Miller-Jones".This wasn't past so instead of being an idiot they opened Chrome and searched Miller-Jones. It led them back to America. This was a huge clue for them. They went to the shop named MJ.Mj stands for Miller-Jones(not Michael Jackson in this story). After going inside they found clothes, not any materials required to make a bomb. George showed a picture of the tag to the owner. Seeing that MJ ran for his life. Again Jackson chased and caught him. While asking him what had happened, George saw the same watch on him. Realizing what could happen he plucked the watch and threw it into a lake behind. As anticipated the watch exploded. The team realized the villain team was always following them. How they realized this was, the watch blasted when they came to detain the man. When they asked who asked him to make the bomb the man ran to the top and jumped off into the lake. They missed this clue too. There was no time to waste. It was a real dead end. Jackson noticed a visiting card lying on the table. While analyzing it they found a familiar name. They were shocked to find out who the person was.

CHAPTER FOUR

Who is behind all of this?

It was none other than Mike. The whole team was shocked. Jackson was puzzled, wondering how such an honest and noble man could be involved in such a sinister plot. Julia, stunned, quickly did a small calculation in her mind, trying to piece together the puzzle. But she had one burning question: Why would Mike try to kill Sarah, his wife? Was it because of his father's position as a general? Determined to uncover the truth, they knew they had to question Mike for answers. So, with resolve in their hearts, they made their way to his house, determined to confront him. They saw him and went up to him. He stayed calm and asked who they were. Mike was shocked that they were just kids below 20 years old but still decided to answer. He asked them how their parents allowed them to adventure. Hearing that Jackson and Julia were sad. Their uncle George revealed that their parents had died in an accident. From then on they have been taken care of by George. Mike hearing it, apologized. The team then told him what was going on. After hearing the whole story, Mike was shocked. He requested them to show the card. After showing it to him, he sat down and started crying. The team was puzzled. After some time, Mike calmed down and began to speak. He revealed that his full name was Jonas Mike and that he was not an only child. He had a brother named Ruke. While Mike was known for being a good and honest person, Ruke was the complete opposite—rude and dishonest. This revelation left the team perplexed, wondering how these two brothers could be so different. Mike continued his story, "When I was 10, I aced my exams, and so did my brother Ruke. However, we later found out that Ruke hadn't earned his grades honestly; he had bribed the teacher. Curious about his sudden wealth, we asked him where he had got the money to bribe, and to our shock, he confessed to robbing someone. As a result, he was homeschooled from then on. When we were 32, there was a bank robbery," Mike narrated, his voice tinged with suspense. "Julia interrupted, asking if it was the infamous Phoedas Bank. Mike nodded, confirming her suspicion. "Yes, it was. During the investigation, we discovered that Ruke and his three friends were the culprits. He was sentenced to 14 years in prison.

Now, I am 40 at present. It's not my name on the card. So is not my father's name which is Richard Mike, as he had passed away 8 years ago. It has written R.Mike instead of J.Mike in the visiting card which is our character's name. (J. Mike stands for Jonas Mike btw.)And my brother still has 6 years to be released."I am unsure what is going on But please find out soon."Said mike. George hearing all of this, asked a question, where is his wife Sarah? He replied that she had been missing for 2 days and thought she had gone back to her home country India for some time. He also said that she would inform him of everything that she does in her plans. She didn't even inform our son, he replied. "He tried to call but she didn't respond, so I complained about this matter to the police", he replied. This indeed is a huge case said George. Geroge remembering about the book that is to be returned, tries to tell the team but Julia and Jackson being busy do not hear it. But when George tries to tell again a maid working there sees him. She asked Geroge whether he was the famous scientist who found a new formula. Confirming this, she gets his autograph and leaves. George after giving his autograph forgot to return the book. Since they had more time till night, the group decided to research about Mike's brother Ruke. They were shocked to find out many criminal activities behind Ruke. They didn't know how Mike's brother Ruke and the Kitsune matter were related. George remembering something went to Julia to tell her. George told her that a few weeks back a top criminal had escaped from jail and told everyone to be safe. Julia was shocked to hear this information. Julia thought that the criminal must be Ruke. But she murmured, "Why did he escape alone without his gang?".Julia asked her uncle, "Do you know how many weeks ago it happened?".Her uncle George replied, "I think around 2 to 3 weeks.".Julia was sure that they had a plan. It was almost 12 late at night. So they went to a room in california and slept. George before sleeping had arranged a small alarm system using a rope and a pan. As expected around 3 AM some people wearing masks came inside and tried to kidnap three of them. I know I know, we all know that Jackson is stronger than Mike Tyso-, I mean at least he is as strong as a bull. So yeah, the pan fell making a huge noise and Jackson beat them so hard they were on the floor begging for mercy. (Probably the thieves were ashamed that they got beaten down by a 15-year-old boy lol.)While asking who had sent them, a familiar name comes out. Who do you think is it? It's none other than Ruke. They realize that Mike was telling the truth. Ruke was behind all of this. But why? The team handed over the men who tried to attack to police. Impressed by them,the police general asked jackson if he wanted to join police after he grew up.Jackson politely declined and said he wanted to do adventures with his sister.

CHAPTER FIVE

Shadowed Peril: Unraveling Truths

In the early light of the next morning, Jackson casually remarked, "My hands feel like they've been punching walls!" (Bro's gotta flex, even in conversation, for the young readers, you know?) Julia and Jackson strolled to their favorite coffee spot, but Julia's senses tingled with a familiar unease—someone was tailing them. Quick on her feet, she spun around, brandishing a pocket knife in a move that would make any shadowy figure think twice. To their relief, it was George, checking in after the previous night's events, ensuring their safety in his own peculiar way. Scaring the team, he simply said, "I feel sleepy." Jackson suddenly asked George if he had drunk the coffee they had brought. George nodded, confirming his theory. Jackson then turned to Julia and inquired if there was a medical lab nearby. Julia, after a moment's thought, replied that there was indeed a lab nearby. Without wasting any time, the team hurried to the lab for answers. Tests revealed that the coffee had been laced with sleeping powder. George, feeling the effects, was overcome with drowsiness. The team decided to retreat to their room, where they stayed until George had fully recovered. The revelation left the team stunned and puzzled. Why had the sleeping powder been mixed into their coffee? Julia realized this was a second kidnap attempt. They were sure that this was done by Ruke too. They then traveled back to India again and met the Army General. They asked him whether his daughter Sarah had come to India and met him. Being confused, he asked, "How did you three come to my house and how do you know my daughter Sarah?" After explaining everything, the general was stunned by two things. One was how two kids below 20 years were able to find out this much without the help of the police. The second was that Sarah hadn't come there either. So where was she? The next minute, the general told his team to search for her and informed the police about the missing case. Then, the Indian police contacted the American police since she had been missing from America, and there was no trace of her coming to India. After an hour, a photograph arrived at the general's desk, revealing a lifeless body lying 40 kilometers away from the Kitsune Shrine. The sight shattered his heart, tears welling in his eyes—it was Sarah. The postmortem report revealed a grim truth: she had been brutally stabbed four times in the neck and shot twice in the head with a small revolver, the gun held so close that it left no doubt. Despite the case being closed as a suicide, Sarah's father was adamant that she could not have taken her own life. Seeking justice, he turned to the group for help in uncovering the truth behind her murder. The group after hearing the fathers cry, were emotional and promised to end this once and for all. After going back to America They informed Mike about Sarah. After telling him, Mike cried for long hours. After he calmed down, he told them that they could ask any help from him. They promised Mike that they would bring Sarah justice and end this once and for all. That time Mike's kid comes in front and plays with Julia and Jackosn without knowing what is going on. Seeing this the whole squad including Mike was heartbroken. George with his team set off to find Ruke. During their research about Ruke, they find out that he is one of the mafia boss's right hand. So he is well hidden. Since they researched and traveled a full, day it's almost 9:30 at night so they go to Georges's home to rest. Suddenly this time, the enemies put a sleep grenade, so even Jackson (The one who is stronger than Mike Tyso-) I mean strong as a bull can't do anything since they got dizzy. After an hour they wake up tied up. The building they are in looks like an old fortress. In front of them is a man sitting on a chair laughing." FOOLS, You know you can't catch Ruke. Why are you even trying?" said the person. He looked like a bull, eyes grey, and his clothes looked like they had been taken from a dump tru-, I mean it was torn and very dirty. They were trapped. They had no way to escape. The man sitting in front ordered his men to kill them and entered a Ferrari. Suddenly Jackson asked time as his last wish to the man. Thinking this as a joke, the man told the time as 11:50. Jackson hearing that, broke his rope and started fighting. Julia understood what he thought, used her pocket knife to cut her rope, and started helping him. George not understanding their intention starts to shout. He shouts that they cannot win against those many people. Julia checks her watch. It is 12:01. Suddenly two helicopters land nearby and a mini army rushes in. The library owner comes slowly walking back. (Must be 69 years old to walk that slow lol). The army shoots everyone there and catches the guy who just flexed his Ferrari. George asked them how they had come here. The owner said, "It's been 3 days aka 72 hours and you haven't returned it.It had a tracker too, So we tracked it and found you guys in this situation. The library owner got his book "The Madness Of The Kitsune" back and dropped them at their home.

CHAPTER SIX

Trap For Ruke.

In their home, the team brainstormed ideas to trap Ruke, the elusive criminal mastermind. As they pondered, George's eyes lit up with a sudden realization. "I've got it!" he exclaimed. "There's a high-profile wedding happening at the museum next week. They'll be showcasing one of the rarest diamonds in the world, but it'll be locked away in a secure alarm box. Ruke won't be able to resist such a tempting target."With their plan in motion, they visited the museum and met with the gracious owner, Rose. She listened intently to their proposal and, impressed by their determination, agreed to assist them in their mission. The stage was set for a showdown with Ruke. They waited for two days. And it was the day for the final show. Sarah's father, the general had his whole team set up for his revenge. As expected Ruke was present there. How the team found it was Ruke is that he was acting weirdly and nervous whenever he went near the diamond box. And he had the same tattoo that Mike had. Everything was set up perfectly. They were waiting for the alarm to ring. Suddenly as they expected the alarm rang. But Ruke was not there. He had already fled with the diamond. Missing the opportunity, the whole team was sad. It was not over yet. The general told them that he was still inside. Julia saw Ruke and started following him. He tried to run but Julia was fast enough to keep on track behind him. He was cornered. Julia saw him for the first time closely. He took out a gun and fired at her. Jackson jumped in between and got the bullet to himself saving her sister. Ruke took this as an opportunity and escaped. Julia cried sitting near her brother. Jackson felt a sharp pain in his side as the bullet tore through his flesh. He staggered, his breath catching in his throat, as he realized he had been shot. Julia's scream echoed in his ears as she rushed to his side, her hands trembling as she tried to staunch the bleeding.In that moment, as he lay wounded and helpless, memories flooded his mind. Memories of their childhood together, of all the adventures they had shared, flashed before his eyes. He remembered the time they had gotten lost in the woods and Julia had refused to leave his side until they found their way home. He remembered her laughter, her smile, and the unwavering courage she always showed in the face of danger.Tears welled up in his eyes as he looked into Julia's eyes, filled with fear and desperation. He knew he had to stay strong, for her sake. With a trembling hand, he reached out and gently caressed her cheek, a silent reassurance that he would be okay. The whole museum went chaotic and rushed Jackson to a hospital. When Julia asked how her brother was, the doctor said it was a miracle that he had survived when a bullet hit his neck. Julia thanked her brother so much for saving her by risking his life. However someone (mhm-) as strong as Mike Tyso-, could not continue to adventure with the team. He needed at least 3 days rest since the bullet hit his skin and not any internal structure. So the team waited till he recovered and started thinking about how to catch Ruke again. While going back to their home, they encountered the kitsune but it looked like it was targeting Jackson. Whenever it attacked, it was targeting Jackson. George being a scientist used a high-frequency device that confused the Kitsune. This allowed them to escape. Julia realized that the kitsune was after the stone they took from the shrine. But why? They had to catch Ruke to get all the answers. They thought of an idea. They planned to make a museum and use it as bait. They asked Rose for help. Since she lost one of her precious diamonds and was kind, she agreed to help. She gave them one of the rarest and fastest cars to use as bait.

CHAPTER SEVEN

The Truth

They advertised and waited for him to come. As expected after two days he came to rob the car. But this time the police surrounded him with arms and caught him. Someone wearing a mask tried shooting Ruke from a bush. Fortunately, the police pulled Ruke towards them so that the bullet wouldn't hit him. Since Jackson could not run because of his injury, Julia ran and caught the person and tore his hand gloves. He somehow escaped from there. But Julia knew who he was since she saw the tattoo. Yes, it was none other than Mike. But she didn't tell the police and kept it a secret. The police caught his neck and pushed him against the wall to handcuff him. Instead of taking him to the station, they took him to Georges's home. There they beat him so hard that he started telling a story. "When Mike and Ruke were around 12 years old, his parents only cared about Mike because he was smart. When I got good marks in all subjects, they told me, I got it on a fluke.

When Ruke was 20 years old, he was in love with a girl named Sarah. However, she had feelings for Mike. In a foolish attempt to win her over, he told her that he was planning to rob a bank. But she betrayed his trust and told Mike about his plan, which ultimately led to his capture. Julia interrupted, asking if Ruke had escaped from jail. He confirmed that he had. "So, that's why you killed Sarah?" Jackson questioned. He replied, "Yes, because of her, I lost 10 years of my life." However, this explanation seemed insufficient. How could this personal vendetta be related to the Kitsune Shrine? He explained that He had been searching for a power stone capable of powering the entire world for millions of years. Ironically, I intended to use it not to empower, but to destroy. He planned to use the stone to create a machine that was 10,000 times more powerful than a nuclear bomb. Jackson was astonished as he continued his story. He revealed that the kitsune had a dark past and had been turned evil. To stop its rampage, the people had no choice but to kill it. Even after its death, the kitsune's heart continued to beat. They removed the heart and transformed it into a stone using Medusa's head. The stone Jackson held was, in fact, the heart of the kitsune. Furthermore, he disclosed that the kitsune following us was a robot under his control. Ruke's initial intention was to use the robot to eliminate Sarah, but thanks to Julia and Jackson's intervention, she was saved. The robot then proceeded to the Kitsune Shrine in an attempt to retrieve the stone, unaware that Julia's team had already obtained it. It targeted Jackson because he possessed the stone. As the tension mounted, the ground beneath began to vibrate. A huge machine came out of the ground and stared at Ruke. Ruke suddenly snatched the stone from Jackson and sat on the head of the machine. He placed the stone and a huge sound came. The machine, so huge with 4 electric claws and a huge blaster, was fully powered up now. If Ruke activated self-destruction, this whole world might disappear. Jackson and Julia had to stop him. But how? Ruke then flew off to the mountains. Julia and Jackson, along with George, sat down to discuss their plan. They knew they had to act fast to prevent Ruke from activating the machine's self-destruction. George suggested that they try to reason with Ruke, to make him see the folly of his plan. Julia was skeptical but agreed to try. They set out to find Ruke, not knowing where he might be hiding. Meanwhile, Ruke was busy making preparations for the machine's activation. He had found a secluded spot in the mountains where he planned to carry out his plan. As he worked, he couldn't shake the feeling that he was being watched. He shrugged it off, attributing it to paranoia. Julia, Jackson, and George searched high and low for Ruke, but he was nowhere to be found. Just as they were about to give up, Julia spotted him in the distance, heading towards the mountains. They followed him discreetly, careful not to alert him to their presence. When they reached the mountains, they saw Ruke standing at the base of the machine, preparing to activate it. Julia stepped forward, calling out to him. Ruke turned a look of surprise on his face. Julia pleaded with him to reconsider, to think about the consequences of his actions. Ruke hesitated, torn between his desire for revenge and the words of reason. This time when Ruke was going to place the stone, a gunshot was heard. The next second, Ruke was lying dead. It was none other than Mike who had shot him.

As the dust settled around Ruke's lifeless body, Julia, Jackson, and George stood in stunned silence. The machine, now devoid of power, loomed over them, a silent testament to the chaos that had nearly been unleashed upon the world. Julia approached Ruke's body, feeling a mix of relief and sadness. Despite his villainous actions, she couldn't help but feel a twinge of sympathy for the man who had been consumed by his thirst for revenge. As they made their way back to civilization, the trio reflected on the events that had transpired. They knew that the world would never be the same, but they also knew that they had played a crucial role in preventing a catastrophe. They had faced danger, betrayal, and loss, but through it all, they had remained steadfast in their determination to do what was right. In the days that followed, the world learned of their heroic deeds. They were hailed as saviors, their names becoming synonymous with courage and selflessness. The presidents of the world gathered to honor them, presenting them with medals and awards for their bravery. But for Julia, Jackson, and George, the true reward was knowing that they had saved countless lives and prevented a disaster of unimaginable proportions. As they looked out at the sunset, their thoughts turned to the future. They knew that there would always be new challenges to face, but they also knew that as long as they stood together, there was nothing they couldn't overcome. And so, hand in hand, they watched as the sun dipped below the horizon, ready to face whatever tomorrow might bring.

www.ingramcontent.com/pod-product-compliance
Lightning Source LLC
Chambersburg PA
CBHW021155130726
47988CB00004B/1620